CHIP ROGERS

COMPUTER WHIZ

CHIP ROGERS
COMPUTER
WHIZ

BY SEYMOUR SIMON

ILLUSTRATED BY STEVE MILLER

WILLIAM MORROW AND COMPANY

NEW YORK   1984

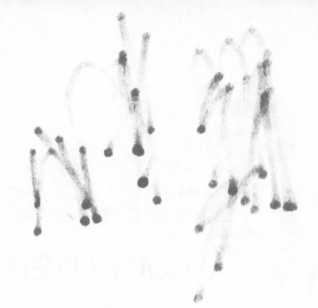

10 9 8 7 6 5 4 3 2 1

Library of Congress Cataloging in Publication Data
Simon, Seymour.   Chip Rogers, computer whiz.

Summary: A computer whiz uses his computer and the help of a
friend to track down a gem robber at the City Museum. Readers
are invited to use their home computers to solve the mystery.
[1. Mystery and detective stories. 2. Computers—Fiction]
I. Miller, Steve (Steve B.), ill.   II. Title.
PZ7.S60573Ch   1984   [Fic]   84-6663
ISBN 0-688-03855-7

To Joyce
with thanks for her patience
with my computer mania


```
NEW
10 REM ACKNOWLEDGMENTS
20 PRINT "SPECIAL THANKS TO
   MICHAEL SANDERS AND JEFF
   ALTMAN"
30 PRINT "FOR THEIR SUGGES-
   TIONS AND HELP WITH THE
   PROGRAMS."
40 END
```

A NOTE TO THE READER

Chip Rogers is for young readers who like to have fun solving a mystery. In it, computer whiz Chip Rogers discovers "whodunit" with the help of a computer. You can use a home computer to solve the mystery, too, because Chip tells you what to do. But you can also match yourself against a computer and solve the mystery just by using your own wits.

Chip Rogers is also for anyone who is interested in computers but knows little about them. In this book, Chip introduces these words, commands, and concepts in using computers and BASIC programs:

```
Bytes              Line numbering
K Bytes            NEW
BREAK              PRINT
Colon              RAM
DIM                REM
END                RETURN
ENTER              RUN
FOR . . . NEXT     Semicolon
INPUT              Strings
LIST               Variable Names
```

CHAPTER
ONE

Would you like to rescue
a 1) princess or a 2) prince?

The words flickered on the TV monitor
screen.

Choose 1 or 2.

Chip Rogers typed the number 1 on the
computer keyboard in front of the screen.

```
    Your goal is to rescue the
princess named Deidre. You
have a long and difficult
journey through mountains,
swamps, and deserts. What
name do you choose for the
leader of your brave group?
(Type name and then press
ENTER or RETURN.)
```

Chip typed "Chip" and then pressed the key marked "ENTER."

The TV screen changed colors from red to blue and back again. Then, in flashing yellow, appeared:

```
Welcome, Sir Chip.
```

Music began to play in the background. It sounded like a slowed-down mechanical version of the theme song from the movie *Rocky*.

"Is that ever corny," Katie Williams said. "Sir Chip! It sounds like a brand of dog food. And suppose I was playing the game and chose my own name for the leader. Do you think that I would really like to be called Sir Katie?"

"I'm just starting to polish up the program and it may have a few bugs in it," Chip admitted with a grin. "But if you had chosen to rescue a prince, the program assumes that the person playing the game is going to rescue someone of the opposite sex. The computer would have called you Lady Katie when you inputed your name. The music needs a little work, too. It sounds as if a record is being played at the wrong speed."

Chip pressed the key marked BREAK and the screen went blank except for the word READY. Then he typed the word LIST and the screen filled with lines of words and numbers that changed rapidly. Chip rubbed his ear in thought. "Let's see," he mused, "I can change the loop that determines the speed of the music and then—"

"Whatever you say, Chip," Katie said. "But why not do it tomorrow? It's very late; it must be ten o'clock. I'm happy that you're teaching computer programming to fifth graders. But, I think I would like to eat something before I go to sleep. Our parents may be worried. It seems as if we've been down here in the City Science and Natural History Museum's computer club room long enough for the dinosaurs upstairs to have become unextinct."

"Is unextinct a word?" Chip asked. "I better look that up in my computer word list. Now where did I put the disc with all those scientific words . . ."

"Chip!" Katie said warningly. "I'm leaving now. Are we going to bike home together or not?"

"Sorry. Sure we'll leave now," Chip said soothingly. "I've got a sort of favor to ask," he continued. "Do you think that I could eat at your house tonight? Mom told me that I would have to make dinner for myself if I got home late, and you know what a disaster that is! I always forget to add something important to the food—like the tuna fish in a tuna fish sandwich. Dad says that he's thinking of changing my nickname from Chip to RAM—Random Access Memory. He says that my memory for food is really becoming random."

"Yes, you can eat at my house tonight," Katie said wearily, "but let's go now without another mention of a computer."

Chip's real name was Charles. He had become interested in computers when he was much younger. Charles was always talking about the chips in computer circuits. A chip is a tiny slice of silicon. It has complex electrical circuits etched on it. It was his dad who first began to call him that when Chip was still in fourth grade. Now that Chip was in eighth grade, he was always writing programs to do such important things as solve math problems, play space adventure games, and keep track of the scoring statistics of the eighth grade basketball team.

Katie Williams was Chip's next door neighbor and best friend. She was two months older and one-and-a-half inches taller than Chip. Katie liked to play the computer games that Chip designed but wasn't too interested in how computers worked. She was a good basketball player and was the manager of the class team.

"The problem with the school computers is that they only have sixteen K memories," Chip said to Katie as they left the basement club room and walked through the darkened halls of the City Museum. "Sixteen K means sixteen thousand bytes, or units of memory. Each byte represents a number or a character. That's not enough memory for a really good game of Dungeons and Dragons. Now with a sixty-four K memory I could program a game that the eighth grade could play all term long."

"Before you do that, how about helping me figure out who to start for Saturday afternoon's basketball game against the ninth grade? We have twelve players on the squad and I'd like to pick out the starting five. It's not easy to choose. Maybe your computer can help me decide—ha, ha."

"Say, that's not a bad idea," said Chip. "I should be able to work out a computer program to choose the players who are most valuable to the team."

"How can you do that?" Katie demanded. "It's not just a matter of who has the best scoring record. You have to consider teamwork and ball handling, too."

"No problem," said Chip. He rubbed his ear. "I'll use different variables for the important factors and weigh each one separately, and then I'll—"

"Don't you ever think of anything besides computers?" Katie asked with a laugh. "Look around," she continued, "we're walking through some of the best displays of gems and minerals you could ever want to see. We've walked through the Hall of Minerals dozens of times on the way to the computer club room downstairs. But I don't think you've ever noticed a single thing about this room."

"Sure I have," Chip said agreeably. "I noticed that it has a ceiling high enough for a basketball court. Of course, the room isn't large enough for a full-court game, but you could put one hoop over there and—"

"Chip!" Katie exclaimed. "Be quiet for a second."

"You know that I'm only kidding," Chip said. "Why are you so excited?"

"It's not you," she said in a whisper. "There's something moving in the shadows over there."

"I guess one of the exhibits came to life." Chip grinned. "Mr. Rock Man has decided to take revenge on the soft people of the world. Or maybe you see an escapee from the snake exhibit. Maybe it's a black mamba or a cobra. Wouldn't that be exciting?"

"There was someone standing in front of

this case of precious gems," Katie said, disregarding Chip's jokes. "I wonder if any are missing." Katie peered into the display case and looked at the gems intently.

"There's something funny about the gems in this case," Katie said excitedly. "You know that I always stop to look at this collection. I looked at them just this afternoon when I went down to the computer club after school."

"So what?" Chip demanded. "Are you telling me that some of the gems are missing?"

"No," Katie said thoughtfully. "But something is wrong. Some of the gems have been switched. Look at that sapphire. It's larger than it was this afternoon, and it's a different shade of blue."

"Which one is that?" Chip asked, and pressed his nose against the glass. "I don't see anything wrong," he said, turning toward Katie.

Suddenly the glass door of the display case that Chip had been pressing against swung open. Chip and Katie looked at each other with astonishment.

"There must be a million dollars worth of gems in this case," Katie said. She pushed against the glass door and it clicked shut. She pushed at the door again but it stayed closed. "We'd better go tell the night watchman."

"Maybe one of us should stay here and the other one get the watchman." Chip was interrupted by a shout from the other end of the room. He looked up and saw a figure running toward them waving a flashlight.

CHAPTER TWO

"What are you two kids doing here?" A museum guard came running up to Chip and Katie. "The museum closes at five o'clock, and all the visitors should be gone."

"We've got permission from the museum director to use the computers downstairs for as long as we want," Chip said. "We were just walking upstairs from the club room. You have to go through the Hall of Minerals to get to the front entrance of the museum."

"Do you have a nighttime pass?" the guard demanded.

Chip and Katie took out museum passes and showed them to the guard. He examined them carefully. "They look okay," he said. "But what are you doing in front of this case of jewels?"

"I thought that I saw someone in the shadows by this display case," Katie said. "But when we came over here there was no one around. Then we looked in the display case and some of the gems seem to be different

12

than they were the last time I saw them."

The guard looked in the display case for several minutes. "None of the jewels are missing," he said. "It's probably just your imagination."

"It's not our imagination that the door to the case was open," Chip replied. "How do you explain that?"

"It was open?" the guard asked. He pushed at the glass door to the display. It remained shut. "The door's not open now," he said.

"But it was open before," Katie said. "We both saw it."

"First you tell me that you saw someone but it was nobody. Then you tell me that there's something different about the jewels, but I can't see anything wrong. Finally, to top it all off, you say that the door to the display case was open but now it's closed and locked. You kids are a nuisance. I'm positive that no one could have opened this case without breaking the glass and setting off an alarm. Nothing happened, get it? I'll walk you to the front door so you can leave." The guard wiped his perspiring face.

"But we really did see something," Katie

said hesitantly as they walked toward the museum entrance.

The guard ran his hand through his gray, thinning hair. "Nobody gets into or out of the museum after hours except through the front entrance and with a museum pass. Everyone who comes in or leaves has to sign the guard book. I walk through each of the museum rooms after closing, and I saw nothing."

"You mean that we're the only ones left in the museum now?" Chip asked.

"No," said the guard. "But everyone who's here now works for the museum and has a pass. There are only two guards on night duty—me and Bill. Bill stays at the entrance whenever I walk around checking the rooms and I stay at the entrance when he walks around. All the windows and side doors are barred and locked. There's no other way in or out at night except past one of us at the front entrance. No one is here at night except some of the museum people who work late."

As Chip, Katie, and the museum guard approached the entrance, they saw another guard sitting on a chair in front of the doors.

"What's up, Frank?" asked the guard at the door.

"Bill, did anyone come in or leave since I began my last tour?"

"Not a soul," Bill said cheerfully. "Why, is there anything wrong?"

"Nothing at all," said Frank. "These kids thought they saw something, but it must have been their imagination." Frank looked at Chip and Katie. "It was a mistake, right?" he asked them.

"I suppose so," Chip said slowly.

"But, Chip—" Katie started to speak.

"Let's talk outside, Katie," Chip interrupted.

Chip and Katie walked out of the entrance and down the wide stone steps in front of the museum. They were silent until they came to the bike rack by the side of the steps. Chip bent down to unlock his bike when Katie stopped him with an angry gesture.

"Chip Rogers, would you mind telling me just why you told the guard that we didn't see anything?" she demanded.

"I didn't exactly say that. I just said that I

supposed so," Chip answered defensively.

"But why didn't you stick to the story?"

"We don't really know if there was someone at the display case or that there's anything wrong with the gems," Chip explained.

"And I suppose that the display door
swinging open was just a dream?" Katie
asked sarcastically.

"No," Chip said, "that wasn't a dream. But
it could have been left open accidentally by
someone working on the gem display. The
alarm didn't go off, and we can't *prove* that
it was open."

"But we could have insisted that the guard call the police or tell the museum director," Katie said.

"That's true," Chip admitted. "But I don't think that we should make things tough for Frank just because we think that something *might* have happened in the gem case."

Katie was silent for a minute. When she spoke her voice was very soft. "That's really very nice of you, Chip. You do think of some things other than computers."

"Yeah, sure," he said in embarrassment.

"But how can we forget about the whole thing?" Katie asked. "Suppose someone really took the gems and put phony ones in their places? I just happened to notice because I thought I saw someone tampering with the display. But it might be a long time till the theft is discovered. Shouldn't we do something?"

"I've been thinking about that," Chip said slowly. "And here's my idea. Why don't we try to find out what's going on by investigating the mystery ourselves? We have passes to be in the museum after hours. We can easily stake out the Hall of Minerals at night. Then we can see if anyone actually is substituting phony gems for the real ones. If we don't see anything, we just forget the whole thing. But if we see anyone tampering with the display, we can tell Frank or the museum director."

"Say, you don't think that Frank could have been the person that I saw in the shadows?" Katie asked thoughtfully.

"Neither Frank nor the guard at the front entrance could have been the person you think you saw," said Chip. "Because if you saw anyone they must have left by the far entrance, near the display case. Frank came from the entrance to the hall near the museum's front door. That's in the other direction. There's no way that he could have gotten around us and come from that direction."

"That's true, Sherlock," Katie said jokingly. "But Frank or the other guard may be the thief's accomplice."

"It doesn't make any difference to our investigation, my dear Watson," said Chip. "We'll be watching the gem display from hiding places. And we'll be able to spot anyone who goes to the case at night."

"But why should the thief come back?"

18

Katie asked. "He's already taken the gems."

"Two reasons," said Chip. "I think that we must have interrupted the thief before he finished. The thief hurriedly shut the door, but the lock didn't click. He's probably not sure if anyone found out. But since there won't be any report about the theft or any police around the museum, the thief will think that no one knows. So he may be back to take more gems tomorrow night or the next night."

"That sounds reasonable," Katie said. "What's the second reason you think the thief might be back?"

"Well, if he wasn't going to steal some more gems why bother substituting phony gems for the real ones? He could have just taken the gems and left the case empty. But he must have wanted the theft to remain undiscovered. And that means that he may come back for more."

"Maybe he works at the museum and is covering up the theft because he might be suspected," Katie said thoughtfully.

"I think that's right," agreed Chip. "Someone who works for the museum would also be able to get in and out at night without causing suspicion. He may also have a key to the display case."

"I just hope that we spot the thief without having him spot us," Katie said. "If he sees us, we could be in big trouble."

"Yeah," said Chip. "And there's something else that's bothering me."

"What's that?" Katie asked.

"My stomach," replied Chip. "I'm hungry. Let's bike back to your house and have dinner."

CHAPTER THREE

After school the next day, Chip was in the basement club room giving an introductory lesson on computers to a small group of fifth graders. Katie had not come downstairs with Chip when they had arrived at the museum. "I have some things I want to see about," she had said to him somewhat mysteriously.

"To make a computer do something, you have to talk to it in a language that it understands." Chip looked at the three boys and two girls clustered around the computer. "Suppose you want the computer to say hello to Tim here. You have to tell it to do exactly that."

"Say, 'Hello, Tim,'" said Tim, a boy with spiky black hair. When nothing happened, Tim said, "Maybe the computer doesn't speak English."

"This computer doesn't understand spoken words," Chip said. "Only special computers do. Nowadays even some small personal computers have attachments that can understand your spoken words. But with this computer, you have to type in the words on a keyboard."

"You mean that's all you have to do—type the words in on the computer keyboard?" asked Nancy, a girl with red hair who was sitting next to Tim.

"Well, you have to tell the computer what to do in a special language called BASIC," Chip explained. "The instructions you give a computer are called a program. We're going to write a simple BASIC program to get the computer to say hello to one of you."

Chip sat down at the computer and typed in this program:

```
NEW
10 PRINT "HELLO, NANCY"
20 PRINT "I AM YOUR FRIENDLY
   COMPUTER"
30 END
```

Chip turned to Nancy. "The word NEW clears the computer's memory of any previous program. Type in the word RUN and then press the key marked ENTER," he said.

Nancy sat down and did as Chip instructed. The screen showed:

```
HELLO, NANCY
I AM YOUR FRIENDLY COMPUTER
```

"Can you make it say hello to me?" Tim asked.

"Can you figure out what kind of change to make in the program?" Chip asked.

"Sure," said Tim. "Just change line ten to read my name."

"That's right," Chip agreed. "Remember to put quotes around the words you want the computer to print."

"Okay," said Tim. "How do I erase the old line ten?"

"Whenever you type in a new line with the same number as an old line, the old line is automatically erased," Chip explained.

Tim typed:

```
10 PRINT "HELLO, TIM"
```

"Now what do I do?" he asked.

"Type RUN and then press ENTER," Chip said.

Tim did, and the screen changed to show his name.

"Do you have to type in a new line every time you want to change a name?" Nancy asked. "That can get boring."

"You're right," Chip agreed. "Here's a

program in which the computer asks your name and fits it in with another line." Chip typed in this program:

```
NEW
10 DIM N$(25)
20 PRINT "WHAT IS YOUR NAME"
30 INPUT N$
40 PRINT "HELLO, ";N$
50 PRINT N$;", YOU AND I
   SHOULD BECOME FRIENDS"
60 END
```

"DIM is short for dimension or the size of the variable that follows," Chip explained. "N stands for the variable name in this program. The dollar sign stands for a group of letters or symbols called a string. I used the number twenty-five in parentheses so that up to twenty-five letters would be accepted. That should be enough for your name. The word INPUT is a way to give the computer information while the program is running. You can use a different name each time you run the program. When the computer gets to the word INPUT it prints a question mark on the screen. Then you type in your name and the computer stores it in the memory and prints it whenever the program shows N string. The semicolon means print N string on the same line. When a semicolon is used at the end of a print statement, the computer stays on the same line of the screen instead of going to the next line."

"Patricia," Chip said, turning toward another girl in the group, "why don't you type RUN and see what happens?"

Patricia went to the computer keyboard. She typed the word RUN and then pressed the key marked ENTER. The screen showed:

```
WHAT IS YOUR NAME
?
```

Patricia typed her name next to the question mark and pressed ENTER. The screen showed:

```
HELLO, PATRICIA
PATRICIA, YOU AND I SHOULD
BECOME FRIENDS
```

"Each time the program is run," said Chip, "it will ask for a name. Then it will fit the name into the two lines that I've programmed. You can program a new name to appear in as many places as you want. Yet you only have to type the name once."

Chip was about to explain some of the other language in the program when he saw Katie enter the room. She motioned for him to come over to her.

"Why don't each of you run the program and input your own name," Chip told the group of children around the computer. "I just want to talk to Katie for a few minutes."

"What's up?" Chip asked.

"I thought that I would try to find out if anyone was working at the museum last night," Katie said. "And I also wanted to see if anything unusual had been reported this morning—like a broken window or something."

"Well, what did you find out?" Chip asked. "Did anyone report something missing from the gem display?"

"I started to talk to the guard who works at the entrance during the day," Katie said, "and he said the same thing Frank did. No one can get in or out of the museum at night except through the front door. It seems that everything is barred and double locked and a burglar alarm goes off if anyone enters through a window or side door. The alarm didn't go off last night, and the windows and doors were checked and found secure. And no one reported missing gems."

"Then we might have been mistaken," Chip said. "Maybe there was no burglary."

"I'm sure that there is something funny going on," Katie said thoughtfully. "I went back to look at the gem display after I talked to the guard. And I'm pretty certain that some of the gems are different from the ones that were in the case yesterday afternoon."

"Did you find out anything else?" Chip asked.

"I found out the names of the people who were in the museum last night," Katie replied. "It seems that there are four museum assistants who work nights on putting together new exhibits. Each one of them was working in a different part of the museum by himself. So any one of them could have opened the gem display and not been seen by the others. It was just the thief's bad luck that we happened to pass by the gem case at the wrong time."

"Were any of them working on a new exhibit in the Mineral Hall?"

"No one was assigned there because there are no new displays. But all of them have worked in the Mineral Hall at one time or another. Maybe one of them was able to get a key to the gem display case."

"Then that person could have made a copy of the key and replaced the original so that nobody would notice," Chip said. "Do you know where each of the assistants is working this week?"

"Here's what I found out," Katie replied.

"Alfred Ball is working on a new exhibit in the Dinosaur Hall. Bernard Carlson is working in the Planetarium. Jordan Marsh and Harry Werner are working in the Hall of Mammals and in the Hall of Birds, but I'm not sure who is working in which place."

"That's not much to go on," said Chip.

"The guard was getting suspicious because I was asking so many questions, so I thought I'd better stop. But I did find out a few more things. The guard mentioned that Marsh and Werner are always arguing. Marsh has long hair and Werner has a crew cut. It seems that Werner is always telling Marsh to get a haircut, and Marsh just keeps laughing at him."

"That doesn't seem to help very much either," Chip said. "It looks like we'll just have to stake out the gem display at night and see if anyone shows up."

"Let's hope that if something happens it happens early enough for us to go home and get some sleep. Tomorrow is Saturday and we have a basketball game scheduled for two o'clock. I haven't even decided who's going to start for our team." Katie paused. "That reminds me," she continued, "last night you said something about a computer program that would help me select the best players. Do you think you could write the program so that I could use it before the game tomorrow?"

"Sure," said Chip. "Let me see how the kids are doing on their programs. Then we'll work on your program. I'll need your help to decide which factors you want to use in making a decision."

"Great," Katie replied. "After the basketball program is done we can go home, then come back to the museum before it closes so that we can hide out in the Mineral Hall."

"Why do we have to go home?" Chip asked. "We might as well stay here until this evening."

"You forgot two things, Mr. Random Memory," Katie said with a smile. "First, if we don't go home and tell our parents where we are, they'll be worried about us. Second, if we don't make some sandwiches and get a few snacks from home, we won't have anything to eat while we're on the stakeout tonight. And I don't think that you can survive staying up all night without food."

Chip grinned and nodded. "The way to a computer expert's brain is through his stomach," he said. "Let's go write the basketball program, Ms. Wise Person."

CHAPTER
FOUR

"There are a few things that we have to decide before we start to write the basketball program," Chip said, rubbing his ear. "First, we have to determine which basketball abilities are most important. Then we can list those abilities as variables and input the information for each player. We'll write the program so that it will assign different scorings to each of the variables, and—"

"Excuse me, Chip," Katie interrupted. "But

would you mind speaking in English instead of computer talk?"

Chip sat down in front of one of the computers in the club room. He smiled at Katie and said, "Sorry, sometimes I get carried away. But it really isn't difficult to write a program to compare basketball skills. Let's do it one step at a time. First, let's decide which basketball abilities are the most important to our team."

"Let's see," Katie said thoughtfully, "shooting is important—you have to make baskets to win games. Dribbling and passing are also important. A good ball handler can usually shoot, dribble, and pass. We need rebounding and defense, of course. And don't forget teamwork. Some kids are good players but always hog the ball. They never pass the ball to anyone else, and they're always shooting. They may score a lot of points, but their team often loses the game."

Chip was taking notes as Katie spoke. "Okay," he said. "Let's see what you think of these variables for the program. First, we'll rate each person in ball handling. That can include shooting, dribbling, and passing. Second, we'll rate each player in rebound-

ing, third in defense, and fourth in team-work. How do those variables sound to you?"

Katie cupped her chin in her hand and thought for a minute. "They sound good," she said. "But some of those things are more important than others. How will the program take care of that?"

"We can assign different weights to each of the variables depending on their importance," Chip said. "You can decide. On a scale of one to four, with four the highest, how would you rate the importance of ball handling?"

"That's very important," Katie said. "I would rate ball handling a four."

"How about rebounding?" Chip asked, taking notes as Katie answered.

"We really don't have much rebounding in our games," she said. "The ball usually bounces around a lot, and the rebound just winds up with whomever happens to be in the right place. I think that I would rate rebounding a two for our team."

"Got it," said Chip. "How about defense? How would you rate the importance of defense on the team?"

Katie was quiet. "I'm not sure," she said after a minute. "Defense is important, but not as important as shooting and ball handling. Suppose we rate defense a three."

"That leaves teamwork," said Chip. "What's the rating you would give for teamwork?"

"Teamwork is very important for any basketball team," Katie said decisively. "I would rate teamwork a four, right up there with ball handling."

Chip looked at his notes and then began to type on the computer keyboard. "First we'll put in some REM statements," he said.

"Whatever you say," Katie agreed. "But

would you mind telling me what you mean by a REM statement?"

"REM stands for remark," Chip explained. "A REM statement is included to help explain the program to a user and also to serve as a reminder to the programmer. The computer doesn't execute a REM statement. It just continues to the next line in the program. You'll only see REM statements when the program is listed on the monitor or printed out on a printer."

Chip continued typing as he talked to Katie. "This should explain the variables," he said, pointing to the monitor screen. The screen showed:

```
NEW
10 REM THIS BASKETBALL
   PROGRAM SHOWS
20 REM WHICH PLAYERS ARE OF
   MOST VALUE
30 REM TO THE 8TH GRADE
   TEAM.
40 REM THERE ARE FOUR
   VARIABLES:
50 REM B=BALL HANDLING
60 REM R=REBOUNDING
70 REM D=DEFENSE
80 REM T=TEAMWORK
```

"There are twelve players on the squad," said Chip. "So the next line tells the computer that each variable will have to be rated twelve times." He typed:

```
90 DIM B(12), R(12), D(12),
   T(12), V(12)
95 REM V=VALUE TO TEAM
```

"Next, we'll have the program print out the information needed by the person who runs the program," Chip said. He typed:

```
100 PRINT "TO USE THIS
    BASKETBALL PROGRAM"
110 PRINT "ASSIGN EACH
    PLAYER A NUMBER"
120 PRINT "FROM 1 TO 12"
130 PRINT "RATE EACH OF THE
    12 PLAYERS"
140 PRINT "FROM 1 TO 4 (4
    BEST)"
150 PRINT "FOR EACH OF THESE
    VARIABLES:"
160 PRINT "BALL HANDLING,
    REBOUNDING,"
170 PRINT "DEFENSE,
    TEAMWORK"
180 PRINT "THE COMPUTER WILL
    SHOW EACH PLAYER'S"
190 PRINT "TOTAL VALUE TO
    THE TEAM"
```

"Now, we'll write the working part of the program," Chip said. "I'm going to use the values that you gave me for each of the four variables." Chip typed:

```
200 FOR I = 1 TO 12
210 PRINT "PLAYER ";I;
220 INPUT
      B(I), R(I), D(I), T(I)
230 NEXT I
240 FOR I = 1 TO 12
250 V(I) = B(I)*4 + R(I)*2
      + D(I)*3 + T(I)*4
260 NEXT I
270 PRINT
280 PRINT "PLAYER'S VALUE TO
      TEAM"
290 PRINT
300 FOR I = 1 TO 12
310 PRINT "VALUE OF ";I;"=";
      V(I)
320 NEXT I
330 END
```

Note: If you have an Atari® computer, you will have to make these changes in the basketball program:

```
220 INPUT B, R, D, T
221 B(I) = B
222 R(I) = R
223 D(I) = D
224 T(I) = T
```

"Now let's run the program," Chip said. He typed the word RUN and pressed the ENTER key. The screen showed the PRINT statements and then the words PLAYER 1?.

"The letter 'I' stands for the players one to twelve. When you see the question mark for each player, you input four numbers for the variables. Use a comma between each number," Chip said. "For example, suppose you rate player one a three in ball handling, a four in rebounding, a two in defense, and a four in teamwork. You would type three comma, four comma, two comma, four and then press ENTER. The screen will then show player two question mark. You enter the information for each of the twelve players and then the computer will show their total value."

"What do all those other words mean?" Katie asked. "And the asterisk?" she added.

"The FOR...NEXT statements tell the computer to repeat some lines in your program as many times as you want. Because you have twelve players you want to rate, the computer will repeat that part of the program twelve times. The asterisk is a com-

40

mand to the computer to multiply the variable by the number that follows.

"Lines 270 and 290 tell the computer to print a blank line. That just makes it easier to read the other lines."

"Do you mind if I run the program myself?" Katie asked. "I want to rate each of the players in private," she explained, "particularly when I rate you. I don't want you peering over my shoulder."

"Go right ahead," said Chip. "I'm sure you'll rate me fairly," he added, "even though I'm your best friend, and I'm the one who wrote this great program. Not to mention the fact that we're going to be on a stakeout tonight in the museum, and our lives may depend on our cooperation."

"I get your point," Katie said with a laugh. "But the total value of each player is up to the computer. So don't blame me for what the computer says your value to the team is."

"I wonder if I created a Frankenstein monster," Chip said, walking away stiffly with his hands stretched out in front of him. "But don't take too long. We have to bike home, make sandwiches, and get back here before

the museum closes for the night. We'll tell
our parents that we'll be working on computers at the museum, and we'll be back very
late. I just hope that I can stay awake all night
long."

"Yeah," Katie agreed. "Let's hope that the
thief decides to come back to the gem case
at the same time tonight as he did last night.
Otherwise we both may fall asleep during the
basketball game tomorrow."

"Maybe I should have put another variable in the basketball program," said Chip.
"Staying awake during the game is defi-
nitely a four."

CHAPTER
FIVE

Chip and Katie got back to the museum a few minutes before closing time. At the entrance the guard waved to them. "I guess you'll be working down in that computer room after-hours," he said with a smile. "I don't understand how those things work," he added. "I just hope that they never find a computer that can do my job."

"Yeah, we'll be working late," said Chip. "And computers aren't so hard to understand. You just have to learn about them like anything else. I hope they won't take people's jobs away but make new jobs. Computers are just tools; it's up to people to use them."

"That's quite a speech," Katie said after they passed beyond the guard's hearing.

"I think I was a little nervous," Chip said. "When I get nervous I begin to talk a lot. You don't think that he was suspicious, do you?"

"That we're bringing sandwiches into the museum?" asked Katie, looking at the bag Chip was carrying. "What could he be suspicious about? Forget about the guard. He goes off duty at six o'clock anyway. Then the night guards come in to work. What do you want to do until then?"

"Let's go downstairs to the computer club room and wait until the museum closes," Chip replied. "We'll come up after they put out the lights. Then we'll find a place to hide near the gem display."

"We really don't have to hide out till about seven or seven-thirty," Katie said. "The four people who work on the exhibits at night don't get here before seven-thirty at the earliest."

"It should be easy to find a place to hide in the Hall of Minerals," Chip said. "They only leave a few lights on at night, and it's pretty dark in the museum. I'm sure that no one will be able to see us."

"It might be a good idea to hide near the museum entrance before the suspects arrive," Katie said thoughtfully. "That way we can see if all four of them are here tonight. There's not much point in hiding out near the gem display if there is no one in the museum working after-hours."

"Good idea," agreed Chip. "Now let's go down to the club room and grab a quick snack. Then we can come back up here by seven-thirty."

"Fine," said Katie. "I'd also like to run the basketball program again. I want to doublecheck the results I got this afternoon."

"Say, that reminds me," said Chip. "Why won't you tell me how the basketball program worked out? Was there anything wrong with the program?"

"No, the program worked fine," said Katie. "But some of the results were a bit surprising. I think that I'd better keep them to myself until the game tomorrow afternoon."

"Whatever you say. Right now I'm more interested in eating anyway," Chip said, rubbing his stomach.

Later, Chip and Katie came back upstairs and hid near the entrance behind a full-size display of a herd of elephants. The elephant display was lighted by two small spotlights, one at either end. In the dim light, the elephants looked huge and menacing. At any moment it seemed as if the front elephant would lead a charge. Chip and Katie were hiding in the shadows behind a baby elephant in the middle of the herd. They could see the museum entrance when they peered around the baby elephant.

"It's funny," Chip said, "but sometimes I think that these elephants are alive and just watching us."

"I know what you mean," Katie said. "The mother elephant just behind us keeps looking at me with a glassy eye."

"That's because her eyes are made of

glass," Chip said. Both he and Katie giggled
nervously.

"We'd better be quiet or the guard will
hear us," Katie said, holding her hand over
Chip's mouth to stop him from giggling. "I

checked with him a few minutes ago. He told me that we were the only ones left in the museum—all the day workers have left."

"Maybe he'll think that the noise is the elephants telling people jokes," Chip said. He and Katie began to giggle harder.

Just then, they heard the guard call out a greeting to someone coming into the museum. Chip peered around the back end of the elephant and Katie peered around the front end. They could just make out a figure talking to the guard at the entrance.

"I'll be working in the Bird Hall tonight," the person said. After a moment, he walked away.

"Do you know who that was?" Chip asked in a whisper.

"No," whispered Katie. "But whoever it is has a crew cut. It may be Werner."

"He's walking up the staircase to the second floor," Chip observed. He was about to add something else when two more people entered the museum.

"Good evening, Mr. Marsh, Mr. Carlson," said the guard to two men who waved as they walked by.

"Do you know which of them is Marsh or Carlson?" Chip asked.

"I don't know any of them by sight," replied Katie.

"Well, one of them is wearing a white shirt and a tie," Chip said. "He seems to be very formal."

"Did you notice that he's also bald?" Katie asked.

"What about the other guy? Can you see anything about him?"

"I can't make him out. He's too much in shadow."

"Well, that makes three out of four that are here," Chip said, rubbing his ear. "I hope that we don't have to wait too long for the fourth person to show up. Maybe one of—"

Chip was interrupted by the guard saying hello to another newcomer. Chip was about to peer around the elephant to see who had come in when he stumbled and fell. Both Chip and Katie froze as they listened to find out if someone had heard the noise.

After a few minutes nothing had happened. They looked toward the entrance but whoever had just arrived had vanished.

"Now what?" Katie asked.

"Let's go around to the different halls and see if any of the suspects are doing anything suspicious," suggested Chip.

"Suppose the thief steals some of the gems while we're watching someone else," Katie said. "One of us should hide out near the gem display, and the other one could scout around."

"That's a good idea," said Chip. "You know the Hall of Minerals better than I do, so why don't you go there? Find a good place to hide so that you can watch the gem display. I'll try to find out what the suspects are doing, and then I'll get back to you."

"Okay," Katie said. "But do it quickly. I don't want to hang around the Hall of Minerals by myself all night long." She waved and walked silently toward the gem room.

Chip turned and walked off in the other direction. "I'll go to the Dinosaur Hall first," he thought. "That's here on the first floor right next to the Planetarium."

Chip walked silently and quickly along a darkened hall that led past many glass display cases filled with assorted bones, minerals, arrow heads, and other museum artifacts. Most of the hall was in deep shadow and Chip was barely able to see where he was going. Once he thought he heard a sound from behind a display case and froze, his heart beating quickly. But after a few minutes nothing happened, and Chip continued along his route.

When Chip got to the Hall of Dinosaurs, he saw that one of the exhibits at the far end was brightly lit. He could see the silhouettes of two people talking to each other in front of the exhibit. One was a man with curly blond hair. The other person was partly hidden and Chip couldn't make out anything about him.

"Will you get a chance to help me tonight, Alfred?" one of the men said. Chip was too far away to see which one was talking.

"Not tonight, Bernard," the other man said. "I'm too busy."

"Those two must be Alfred Ball and Bernard Carlson," Chip thought. "I'd better get along and see if I can spot the other two suspects before Katie gets too nervous."

Chip backed out of the Dinosaur Hall very

quietly and continued walking toward the Planetarium. Its big double doors were closed. He tried pushing them open, but they were locked. Chip put his ear to the doors but heard nothing so he pressed on to the Hall of Mammals. He saw no one walking around the corridors.

When Chip got to the Hall of Mammals, he saw someone standing on a ladder next to a model of a gorilla. The person was wearing a brightly flowered shirt. Chip watched him for a minute or two, then decided to move on to the Hall of Birds, which was up on the second floor of the museum.

Chip found the staircase at the end of the hall and peered up. The top of the staircase was completely in the dark, and he could see nothing. "Maybe I should get back to Katie now," Chip said silently. "Don't be a chicken, Sir Chip," he told himself. "There's nothing up there."

Chip cautiously walked up one step at a time. When he got to the second floor, he blundered into a display case and lost his way in the dark. It took him nearly fifteen minutes to make out where he was. He wandered through the Hall of Reptiles and the Hall of Amphibians before he found the Hall of Birds. He was about to go in when he saw a person wearing a blue shirt walk into the Bird Hall. Chip quickly ducked behind a display case full of birds' eggs.

Chip couldn't see into the hall, but he could hear the sound of two voices. Two men were calling each other Jordan and Harry. "They must be Jordan Marsh and Harry Werner," Chip said to himself. "That means that all four suspects are here in the museum. I'd better get back to Katie now," he decided.

Chip found his way back to the dark staircase and silently crept down the stairs to the first floor. Every few steps he stood still and peered vainly through the dark. The museum around him seemed full of lurking figures and odd noises. "It's just your imagination," Chip told himself, but his heart was pounding nevertheless.

Chip was almost at the entrance to the Hall of Minerals when he heard a strange sound in front of him. It sounded like a laugh that was choked back. "That must be Katie," he assured himself. "She's still giggling. She must be at the other end of the hall near the gem display. Why isn't she quieter? Someone will hear her."

Chip was about to creep into the Mineral Hall to find Katie when he felt a hand grab his shoulder and pull him around. *"Uhr-ug!"* Chip exclaimed.

CHAPTER SIX

"*Sshhh,*" Katie said. "Did I startle you?"

"Not too much," Chip said with a weak smile.

"Then do you mind telling me what 'uhr-ug' means?" she asked innocently.

"Did I say that? I guess I was a bit startled." Chip looked around the Hall of Minerals. "You must have found a good hiding place. I couldn't see you at all when I came in."

"I was hiding behind the igneous-rock exhibit over there. The problem is that I can only see one entrance to the hall from where I'm hiding. The other entrance is hidden behind some of the other exhibits. The gem display case is also pretty much in shadow. I think it would be better if one of us hid near each entrance. That way one of us will see whoever comes."

Chip nodded. "Okay. I'll go find a hiding place by the other entrance."

"Just a minute," Katie said. "Before you disappear, would you tell me what you found out on your travels through the museum?"

"I didn't find out much. All four of our suspects are working here tonight. I jotted down everything I saw in my notebook, but I don't know if it will be of any help. Unless we can see the thief come back to the gem case, I think we're out of luck."

Katie frowned. "You're probably right. But we may not even recognize the thief if we do see him. We don't know what our four suspects look like. And I don't think that we should try to stop the thief if he does come back. He may be violent."

Chip rubbed his ear. "Let's worry about

57

that if we have to. We'll just watch and see what happens and then report what we saw to the museum director. Right now I'm going to find a good hiding place."

Chip trotted over to the other end of the hall. He looked around and finally selected an enormous quartz crystal near the entrance. Chip crouched down behind it. He could easily see the entrance when he peered around the side of the crystal. The gem display case was more difficult to see because it was in shadow and at a bad angle. Chip looked down to the other entrance of the hall, but he could not spot Katie.

Chip settled himself comfortably behind the crystal. He took out his notebook to look at the notes he had made of the things he had found out about each of the suspects.

Suddenly a thought occurred to him. All the facts and observations about the suspects could be entered in a computer program. The program would correlate the facts that Katie had found out from the guard and the observations they made tonight. "It'll give me something to do while I'm waiting," Chip thought.

Chip began to write in his notebook. After

he filled two pages with a program, he stretched and yawned. The program would fill in some of the unknown facts about the suspects, but so far there wasn't enough to determine the thief's identity. Chip decided that he might as well work on his new adventure-game program.

Chip was trying to program a tricky spot involving a three-headed monster named Ghidrah. Ghidrah could either be tamed with the right words or would attack if the wrong words were chosen. Chip was becoming sleepier and sleepier.

He closed his notebook and settled back against the quartz crystal. The last thought he had before he dozed off was that Ghidrah would make a marvelous basketball player. His three heads could look in different directions at the same time. And his fiery breath was sure to discourage his opponents.

Chip woke up to the loud click of a lock snapping shut. For a few seconds he couldn't remember where he was. Then his heart sank. While he was sleeping, someone must have entered the hall.

Chip peered around the side of the quartz

crystal. Sure enough, there *was* someone in front of the gem display case. But the figure was too much in shadow for Chip to get a good look at the face.

Suddenly, the figure started to walk away from the case and toward the entrance near Chip. His path would take him only a few feet away. Chip crouched down behind the crystal and tried to make himself as small as possible. If he looked out, the thief would surely see him! The sound of footsteps came

closer and then began to recede. The thief was walking away, and Chip hadn't even seen who it was.

Chip stood up cautiously and looked toward the entrance to the hall. Someone carrying a small black bag was hurrying away. Besides the bag the only other thing Chip noticed was that the person was wearing a red shirt.

Chip tiptoed into the corridor and looked down the dimly lit passage leading to the front entrance. The figure was nowhere in sight. Chip was deciding whether to follow down the hallway when he heard Katie calling to him.

Katie ran toward Chip. "Did you see the thief? He came through the entrance near you and was at the gem display case for ten minutes. He must have substituted fakes for a lot more of the gems. Now we know that there really was a robbery, and we can even identify the thief. You must have gotten a good look at his face. Right?"

"Well, the truth is that I didn't exactly get a good look at him." Chip looked embarrassed.

"Why not? You must have seen him from where you were hiding."

"I sort of fell asleep," Chip admitted.

Katie was incredulous. "You fell asleep! Didn't you see anything?"

"Oh sure. I saw that the thief was carrying a black bag."

"Yes," Katie said impatiently, "and what else did you see?"

"That's about all I saw. Except that he was wearing a red shirt."

Katie was furious. "That's just great. Now we know that the thief was carrying a black bag and was wearing a red shirt. How is that going to help us identify him? Do you think he always wears a red shirt and carries a black bag? Not likely! Let's take a look at the gem display and see if we can spot anything."

Chip and Katie went over to the display case and looked inside. Chip tried to open the door of the case, but it was locked. "Do you notice anything different?" he asked.

Katie looked at the gems carefully. "That sapphire is different and that ruby looks different, too," she said. Katie continued looking. "There are some other gems in the case that look as if they might be different than the ones that were here before, but I'm not sure."

Katie turned to Chip. "We have to tell the museum director about the theft. We should have told him right away. We can say that we suspect one of the four people who work on the exhibits at night."

"Why should the director believe us?" Chip asked. "If gems were substituted, he might even suspect that we did it. After all, we were in the Hall of Minerals both nights. No, we have to go to the director after we find out who the thief is."

"How can we tell who the thief is when you fell asleep and didn't get a good look at him?" Katie demanded.

"All we have to do is find out which of the four suspects wore a red shirt tonight," Chip said. "When we know that, we'll know who the thief is."

"How do you expect to find that out? The night workers must have left the museum by now. The thief probably took the gems just before they were all scheduled to go home.

And if we question everybody, it will alert the thief and he will deny everything and destroy the evidence."

"I think that I can find out who was wearing a red shirt without asking anyone," Chip said. "Follow me."

"Where are we going?" Katie asked as she walked with Chip. "Where do you expect to find the suspect with the red shirt?"

"Why, in the computer club room, of course," he replied.

CHAPTER SEVEN

Chip snapped on the light switch in the computer club room. He walked over to a chair and sat down beside a desk cluttered with cables, floppy disks, special connectors, and other assorted computer items. Chip pushed them to one side and beckoned Katie to sit down next to him. He handed her a pencil and paper.

"I want you to jot down everything that we've found out about the theft," Chip said.

"I'll do the same. Then we'll combine our notes and see what we know and what we have found out."

Katie shook her head. "I'll do what you say, but I don't see what good it will do. We didn't see who the thief was. And what good are all the other things we found out? Besides, I thought you were going to use a computer to find the thief. Why are we using a paper and pencil?"

"We'll use a computer later," Chip said. "But a computer will help you only if you program it correctly. To do that, we have to tell it exactly what we want it to do. We also have to present our instructions to the computer in its own language. So just write down what you know about the theft and about the suspects."

"It's easy to find out what we know," said Katie. "But what we *don't* know is who did it."

"You mean whodunnit," Chip said with a grin. "That's what we professional detectives say. Seriously, just go along with me on this and let's see what happens."

Katie nodded in agreement and both got to work. After about ten minutes they finished their lists. Chip took the two lists and placed them side by side. Then he began to make a single list that eliminated duplications.

Katie looked at the list as Chip wrote.

What We Know
1. There are four suspects: Alfred Ball, Jordan Marsh, Harry Werner, and Bernard Carlson.
2. Alfred Ball has been working in the Hall of Dinosaurs.

3. Bernard Carlson has been working in the Planetarium.
4. Jordan Marsh has long hair.
5. Harry Werner has a crew cut.
6. Marsh and Werner argue about Marsh's long hair.

What We Saw
1. The thief wore a red shirt.
2. The thief carried a black bag.
3. The suspect working in the Hall of Birds had a crew cut.
4. Either Marsh or Carlson was wearing a white shirt and tie.
5. The suspect wearing a white shirt and tie was bald.
6. Ball and Carlson were seen talking together in the Dinosaur Hall.
7. Either Ball or Carlson has curly blond hair.
8. The suspect working in the Hall of Mammals was wearing a flowered shirt.
9. Marsh and Werner were heard talking together in the Hall of Birds.
10. One of the men in the Hall of Birds was wearing a blue shirt.

Katie looked at the list and shook her head in puzzlement. "We'll never figure out who the thief is with this list. We should have told the museum director about the theft last night. At least we could have prevented more gems from being taken. All these clues don't add up to anything."

"That's where you're wrong," Chip said. "Not all of the clues are important, but some are very important. And there are probably enough of them now to show you who the thief is. If you are very logical and keep all the details in mind, it would be possible— without a computer—to figure out who stole the gems. But a computer has a perfect memory and is very fast at logical reasoning. If it is programmed with the clues we found out, it can be told to keep trying them until it knows the name of the thief."

"That I have to see," said Katie, shaking her head doubtfully.

"I'd already started to write the program while I was hiding in the Hall of Minerals," said Chip. "It won't take me too long to write the rest."

Chip went over to one of the museum's computers and turned it on. He began to type. From time to time he stopped and rubbed his ear in thought. Then he started typing again. Almost an hour passed before Chip looked up from the keyboard of the computer. Katie had fallen asleep.

Chip gently shook her shoulder. "Wake up, Katie. I've finished writing the program. I thought you would like to run it and see if we can find out who the thief is."

Katie yawned and rubbed her eyes. "It's almost worth waking up for that," she said.

Chip handed her a printout of the program. "The program is already entered in the computer. All you have to do is type the word RUN and press the ENTER key. The name of the thief will appear on the screen. You can see the clues I use by the REM statements."

Katie looked at the program. "I see that you didn't use many of the observations we listed," she said. "How did you decide which ones to use?"

"I knew that we had to find out who wore the red shirt," Chip explained. "So I used the kinds of clues that would lead to that person. That meant that I would try to find out about the suspects' looks—how their hair looked. Also important were the suspects' clothing, and where the suspects were working. The other clues were not useful. For example, the observation that the thief carried a black bag did not help us in any way."

Katie looked at the program again. "What does this mark mean?" She pointed at a mark that looked like this: < >

"That means that what follows is not true or equal," Chip explained. "The equal sign means that the statement is true. Every time you see a line that begins REM, it means that it is a remark. The remarks help explain what's happening in the program. The colon just separates different statements on the same line."

Here is the program that Chip wrote:

```
NEW
1 REM THIS PROGRAM IS
   WRITTEN TO FIND THE GEM
   THIEF IN THE
2 REM CITY MUSEUM WHO WORE A
   RED SHIRT.
10 DIM C(4,3)
20 REM C IS THE ARRAY FOR
   THE CLUES.
30 REM THE 4 STANDS FOR THE
   NUMBER OF SUSPECTS.
40 REM 1=ALFRED BALL
   2=JORDAN MARSH
50 REM 3=HARRY WERNER
   4=BERNARD CARLSON
60 REM THE 3 STANDS FOR THE
   KINDS OF CLUES.
70 REM THE THREE KINDS OF
   CLUES ARE: 1=WORKROOM,
   2=LOOKS, 3=CLOTHING.
```

```
80 REM THE WORKROOMS ARE:
   1=DINOSAUR ROOM,
   2=PLANETARIUM
90 REM 3=MAMMAL ROOM,
   4=BIRD ROOM.
100 REM LOOKS ARE: 1=LONG
    HAIR, 2=CREW CUT
110 REM 3=CURLY BLOND HAIR,
    4=BALD.
120 REM CLOTHING IS:
    1=FLOWERED SHIRT,
    2=WHITE SHIRT
130 REM 3=BLUE SHIRT, 4=RED
    SHIRT.
140 FOR X=1 TO 4:FOR Y=1 TO
    3:C(X,Y)=0:NEXT Y:NEXT
    X:REM X=SUSPECTS,Y=KINDS
    OF CLUES, 0=UNKNOWN
150 REM SET KNOWN CLUES
160 C(1,1)=1:REM ALFRED
    BALL WORKS IN THE
    DINOSAUR ROOM.
170 C(2,2)=1:REM JORDAN
    MARSH HAS LONG HAIR.
180 C(3,2)=2:REM HARRY
    WERNER HAS A CREW CUT.
190 C(4,1)=2:REM BERNARD
    CARLSON WORKS IN THE
    PLANETARIUM.
```

```
200 REM USE THE OBSERVED
    CLUES TO FIND THE THIEF.
210 FOR X = 1 TO 4
220 IF C(X,2)=2 THEN 250
230 NEXT X
240 GOTO 800
250 C(X,1)=4:REM THE
    SUSPECT IN THE BIRD HALL
    HAD A CREW CUT.
260 FOR X = 1 TO 4
270 IF C(X,1)=0 THEN 300
280 NEXT X
290 GOTO 800
300 C(X,1)=3:REM HAVING
    FOUND THE WORKROOMS OF
    THREE SUSPECTS,
    ELIMINATION FINDS THE
    WORKROOM OF THE FOURTH.
310 FOR X = 1 TO 4
320 IF C(X,1)=3 THEN 350
330 NEXT X
340 GOTO 800
350 C(X,3)=1:REM THE
    SUSPECT WORKING IN THE
    MAMMAL HALL WORE A
    FLOWERED SHIRT.
360 IF C(4,3)=1 THEN
    C(2,3)=2:REM IF CARLSON
    IS WEARING A FLOWERED
    SHIRT, THEN MARSH'S MUST
    BE WHITE.
```
74

```
370 IF C(2,3)=1 THEN
    C(4,3)=2:REM IF MARSH
    IS WEARING A FLOWERED
    SHIRT, THEN CARLSON'S
    MUST BE WHITE.
380 REM EITHER CARLSON OR
    MARSH WORE A WHITE SHIRT.
390 REM IF WE KNOW THE COLOR
    OF ONE OF THEIR SHIRTS,
    WE CAN FIND THE SECOND
    BY ELIMINATION.
400 IF C(2,3)<>0 AND
    C(3,3)<>0 THEN 800:REM
    IF BOTH SHIRTS ARE KNOWN,
    THIS IS THE WRONG PATH
    TO FOLLOW.
410 IF C(2,3)=0 AND C(3,3)=0
    THEN 800:REM IF BOTH
    SHIRTS ARE UNKNOWN, THIS
    IS THE WRONG PATH TO
    FOLLOW.
420 IF C(3,3)<>0 THEN
    C(2,3)=3:REM IF
    WERNER'S SHIRT IS KNOWN,
    THEN MARSH'S SHIRT MUST
    BE BLUE.
430 REM MARSH AND WERNER
    WERE IN THE BIRD HALL.
440 REM ONE OF THE SUSPECTS
    IN THE BIRD HALL WAS
    WEARING BLUE.
```

```
450 FOR X=1 TO 4:IF
    C(X,3)=0 THEN 470:NEXT
    X
460 GOTO 700
470 C(X,3)=4:REM IF THREE
    SHIRTS ARE KNOWN, THEN
    THE FOURTH CAN BE FOUND
    BY ELIMINATION.
510 FOR X=1 TO 4:IF
    C(X,3)=4 THEN 550
520 NEXT X
530 GOTO 800
540 REM THE SUSPECT WEARING
    THE RED SHIRT IS THE
    THIEF.
550 PRINT "THE THIEF IS ";
560 ON X GOTO
    580,600,620,640:REM THE
    PROGRAM GOES TO THE
    CORRECT NAME.
570 PRINT "ERROR STOP":END
580 PRINT "ALFRED BALL!"
590 END
600 PRINT "JORDAN MARSH!"
610 END
620 PRINT "HARRY WERNER!"
630 END
640 PRINT "BERNARD CARLSON!"
650 END
```

```
700  PRINT "THERE ARE NOT
     ENOUGH CLUES AT THIS
     TIME TO DEDUCE THE
     THIEF."
710  END
800  PRINT "THE WRONG PATH
     OF LOGIC IS BEING
     FOLLOWED."
810  END
```

TO THE READER: Can you figure out who the thief is? You can reason it out without a computer. You can also find out by running this program on most home computers, including APPLE®, ATARI®, COMMODORE®, TRS 80®, and IBM PC*jr*®. It will run on other home computers if you make slight changes in the language. Consult your computer guide.

CHAPTER EIGHT

Early the next morning, Chip and Katie went to the museum director's office. They were both sleepy but very excited. They knocked on the office door, and a voice from inside told them to enter.

The museum director was sitting behind a large, wooden desk. Books, papers, and magazines were spread out in front of him. The floor was also heaped with piles of books in unsteady stacks. The walls of the office were covered with photographs and paintings. Most of the photographs were of people and animals. All of the paintings were of animals except for one of a person who looked like the director.

The director had a round, red face and a fringe of a red beard. He wore a pair of wire rim glasses. His face broke into a smile when he saw Chip and Katie.

The director took off his glasses and placed them on top of a stack of papers on his desk. "What have we here?" he said. "You're the children helping us to give computer courses in the basement. The computer club room has become one of the most popular attractions in the museum. I want to thank you both for your work here."

"You're welcome," said Chip. "I really enjoy working with computers and—"

Katie interrupted him. "But that's not why we're here," she said. "There's been a gem theft in the museum, and we know who did it." She glanced at Chip. "I mean, we know whodunnit."

The director stopped smiling. He looked sternly at Chip and Katie. "What do you mean?" he demanded.

Katie told the director the story of how they had first noticed the theft. She explained how the display door had swung open and then locked. She said that she often looked at the gems and was sure that some looked different than they had before.

"I haven't noticed anything different in the gem display," the director said. "Are you sure that you're not just imagining the whole thing?"

"At first we weren't sure," Chip said. "But now we know that there was a theft and that the thief substituted phony gems for the real ones." Chip went on to explain what had happened in the museum last night.

"But you say that you never got a look at the thief," the director said. He looked puzzled. "All you saw was that he wore a red shirt."

"I used a computer to help find out the thief," Chip explained. "I wrote a program using all the information we learned and the things we observed. The computer came up with the name of the person who wore a red shirt. And that person is the thief."

"And who is that?"

"The thief who wore the red shirt last night is Alfred Ball," Chip said.

"Alfred Ball!" The director was startled. "He's been working in the Hall of Dinosaurs. But wait a minute. Ball does have a knowledge of gems. And he was working in the Hall of Minerals last month." He picked up his glasses. "You two stay right here till I get back. We'll soon get to the bottom of this."

The director left his office and closed the door behind him firmly. Chip and Katie looked at each other.

"I hope he comes back soon," Katie said.

"We have to play basketball in a few hours."

"Maybe we can take a nap until he gets back," Chip suggested. "We didn't get much sleep last night and I'm tired."

"Good idea," Katie agreed. She looked around the office. "Let's just move some of those piles of books onto the floor so we can have some room."

Chip and Katie moved some of the books away and were soon asleep. It seemed like only a few minutes before they were awakened by the director coming into the office.

He was smiling. "I want to thank you both for everything that you've done. I went to check the gem display with an expert in gems and minerals. He picked out twelve phony gems. You were absolutely right. Then I notified the police. They went to Alfred Ball's house with a warrant and found the gems and a duplicate key to the gem display case. Ball substituted phony gems for the real ones. He was going to quit his job, leave town, and sell the gems. He thought that no one would notice that the real gems were gone until it was too late."

"I'm glad he was caught before he could

get away. But can we go now?" Katie said. "Our class has a basketball game this afternoon."

"Of course you can go," the director said. "And when you come back here on Monday to give your introductory computer course, you're going to have a new student—me."

Chip turned to Katie as they were leaving the museum. "You never told me what happened when you tried out my basketball program," he said.

Katie looked embarrassed. "I just used the program the way you told me. It's not my

fault that you weren't one of the starting five players."

"What?!" Chip was indignant. Then he relaxed and rubbed his ear. "I guess I'll just have to write a different basketball program for you to use next time," he said with a smile.

ABOUT THE AUTHOR

SEYMOUR SIMON is the author of more than eighty science books for children, including *Hidden Worlds, Little Giants,* and *The Optical Illusion Book,* as well as *The Long Journey from Space* and the *Einstein Anderson* series of science mystery stories. He is also writing a series of introductory books on computers and enjoys working on several different computers at home.

He and his wife live in Great Neck, New York.

ABOUT THE ILLUSTRATOR

STEVE MILLER's cartoons have appeared in *The New York Times, The Washington Post,* and *Time* magazine. He has also written and illustrated stories for such prominent magazines as *Esquire, Playboy,* and *National Lampoon,* and is the author/illustrator of *The Midnight Son.* Recently, he illustrated *"The Earth is Flat"—and Other Great Mistakes* for Morrow Junior Books.

Steve Miller lives and works in New York City.